D1325593

The Return of the Young Prince

The Return of the Young Prince

A.G. Roemmers

Illustrated by Pietari Posti

Translated from the Spanish
by Oliver Brock

ONEWORLD

Visit our website for exclusive content on

The Return of the Young Prince

www.oneworld-publications.com

Foreword

Some years ago, during a brief stay in Buenos Aires, I was lucky enough to meet Alejandro Guillermo Roemmers. I had told my cousins, François and Jean d'Agay, Saint-Exupéry's nephews, that I wanted to trace the route of the pilots who had made the Aéropostale company's first stops in Argentina and Chile. They gave me Roemmers's details straight away and told me to get in touch with him. I called him as soon as I got to Argentina and we agreed to have dinner. It was late that night that I first heard about *The Return of the Young Prince*.

We talked all evening, and I came away with a copy of his book, ready to start my journey through Patagonia and the Andes. When I opened it, I found an introduction to the first Argentinian edition by

Frédéric d'Agay, Saint-Exupéry's great-nephew, and at that time president of the Antoine de Saint-Exupéry Youth Foundation, which said, 'Alejandro Roemmers held on to the spirit of his inner child, and when he met his Little Prince in Argentina, he wanted to relate that to us with this story, and draw our attention to its essence, to the poetry of it.'

Frédéric was right. Roemmers, as well as being a renowned poet, is a businessman who spends a lot of his time travelling – much of it in response to invitations to present his book and his ideas. He visits schools, colleges and universities, promoting his message: namely that with education, faith, courage and temperance, it is possible to beat poverty, illiteracy and cynicism. He also gives special importance to the redemptive power of love, and how it can help us confront the erosion of values in today's world.

This book is the story of the Young Prince's journey through the desolate, deserted landscapes of Patagonia, and how that affords a privileged adult the opportunity to engage with a teenager, who has come out of nowhere and will encourage him to move beyond appearances. It is a sort of initiation journey of youth, and a return to first principles for any adult who might feel uprooted.

At times, *The Return of the Young Prince* can read

like a contemporary catechism, written in the twenty-first century by a man buoyed by his ambition for great changes in a society that is rejecting inadequate political structures and that won't risk an education system capable of instilling a message of hope.

This book reminds us of the values we should never have abandoned: the importance of friendship, family, community, and compassion – the pillars of every civilised society.

Through his hero, the poet and author shows us how, with their courage, their temperance, their vision for the world and sometimes even with their lives, certain men – like those who brought glory to the Aéropostale company, its great pilot Antoine de Saint-Exupéry above all – told us the way to go.

The Return of the Young Prince lights the way for us and helps us to champion the magic of love, its capacity to change everything.

Bruno d'Agay
A member of the Saint-Exupéry family

A Few Words by Way of Introduction

In a world that was ravaged by war and rapidly losing its innocence and joy, the intrepid French aviator Antoine de Saint-Exupéry wrote *The Little Prince*. It would soon become the universal symbol for those lost values.

Saint-Exupéry's sadness and disillusion in an era that seemed to be forgetting the simplicity of the heart, and humanity's profound spirituality, were more likely than any burst of enemy fire to have been the cause of his untimely disappearance on a reconnaissance mission over the Mediterranean.

Like many others who have read *The Little Prince*, the purity of its message resonated with me, and I shared in Saint-Exupéry's sadness when that child, who had found a place so deep in my heart, had no choice but to go back to his asteroid.

It was only some time later that I understood that hatred, a lack of understanding and solidarity, a materialistic view of the world and other negative forces would have prevented him from living among us in any case.

Many times I have asked myself, as perhaps you have: what would have become of that very special child had he continued to live on our planet? What would his adolescence have been like? How would he have held on to the purity of his heart?

It has taken me many years to find answers to these questions, and even then it's possible that they are only of value to me. But my hope is that they might at least shine some light on the path towards celebrating the child that each of us carries inside.

And so I presume to write to you, dear reader, at the start of a new century and a new millennium, with a more positive vision of our time, so that you might not be so sad.

I'm sorry not to satisfy your curiosity if you were expecting a photograph of him – many years ago I stopped taking any kind of camera on my journeys, especially since I noticed that my friends would focus so much on the pictures that they stopped listening to the stories that went with them. However, I've included a few drawings so that you won't think this story too serious. After various attempts of my own that would have satisfied neither adult nor child, we decided to ask Pietari Posti for help in recreating some of the moments I remember most vividly. Don't let his lines lead your imagination, as he hasn't been to Patagonia, nor has he met the mysterious boy of this story; but perhaps they will help you see inside my words, just like the Little Prince could see the sheep inside its box...

Lastly, dear reader, I hope you will forgive me for including here my own thoughts and reflections that arose as these things happened – I wanted to honour them by writing a faithful record.

And now, I'm going to tell you the story exactly as it happened.

If you feel alone, and if your heart is pure and your eyes still shine with the wonder of a child's, perhaps as you read these pages you'll find that the stars are smiling on you once more, that you can hear them as though they were five hundred million little bells.

Chapter One

I was driving alone down a lonely road in Patagonia – a land named after an indigenous tribe you could supposedly spot by their disproportionately large feet – when I suddenly saw a strange shape to one side of the road. I slowed down instinctively, and was amazed when I saw a lock of blond hair poking out from under a blanket that seemed to conceal a person. I stopped the car, and when I got out I saw something astonishing. All the way out there in the middle of the plain, hundreds of miles from the nearest town and without so much as a single house, a single tree or fence post in sight, a boy was sleeping peacefully without a care in the world.

What I'd wrongly taken for a blanket was in fact a long blue cape, with epaulettes and a purple lining you could just glimpse, with a pair of white trousers like jodhpurs emerging from underneath it, tucked into boots of shining black leather.

The whole thing gave the boy a princely sort of air that was out of place around those parts. A straw-coloured scarf, fluttering nonchalantly in the spring breeze, blended sometimes with his hair, giving him a melancholic, dreamy look.

I stood there for a while, baffled by what seemed a complete mystery. It was as though even the wind, as it swept down in great gusting dust clouds from the mountain, had skirted politely around him.

I understood straight away that I couldn't leave him there, asleep and defenceless in that solitary place and without food or water. Even though nothing about his appearance was frightening in the least, there was a certain resistance I had to overcome before approaching the stranger. With some difficulty, I gathered him up in my arms and laid him down in the passenger seat.

The fact that he hadn't woken up seemed so odd that for a moment I feared he might be dead. A weak yet constant pulse proved he wasn't. As I placed his limp hand back on the seat, I thought that if I hadn't seen so many images of winged creatures, I might have believed I was in the presence of an angel come down to Earth. I soon realized the boy was exhausted, at the end of his strength.

Back on the road, I spent a long while thinking about how all those warnings designed to protect

us as adults, in fact distance us so much from others that touching someone or even looking them in the eye has us uncomfortable and anxious.

'I'm thirsty,' the boy said suddenly, and I jumped because I'd almost forgotten he was there. Even though he had spoken very softly, the sound of his voice was as clear as the water he was asking for.

On long journeys like that one, which could last up to three days, I always packed drinks and something to eat in the car so that I didn't have to stop other than to fill up with petrol. I gave him a bottle, a plastic cup and a beef-and-tomato sandwich wrapped in foil. He ate and drank without saying a word. Meanwhile, my head was starting to teem with questions: 'Where are you from? How did you get here? What were you doing lying by the road like that? Do you have a family? Where are they?' And so on and so forth.

Considering my anxious nature, and that I'm always brimming with curiosity and the wish to help, I'm still amazed I was able to stay quiet for those ten endless minutes while I waited for the boy to get his strength back. He, on the other hand, tucked into his meal like it was the most normal thing in the world, after lying abandoned in the middle of those desert-like plains, for someone to appear out of the blue and offer him a drink and a beef-and-tomato sandwich.

'Thank you,' he said as he finished, before leaning back against the window, as though that word was enough to answer all my doubts.

A moment later I realized I hadn't even asked him where he was heading. As I'd found him on the right-hand side of the road, I'd taken it for granted that he was travelling south, but in fact it was much more likely he was trying to get to the capital, which lay to the north.

It's strange how easily we assume that others must be going in the same direction as us.

When I looked over at him, it was too late. Other dreams had come and carried him a long way off.

Chapter Two

Should I wake him up? No, we needed to cover some ground; whether we went north or south was of little importance.

I sped up. This time I wouldn't waste any more of my life asking myself what direction to go in.

I was absorbed in these thoughts when, after a long time had passed, I suddenly felt a pair of blue eyes watching me curiously.

'Hi there,' I greeted him, turning briefly towards the mysterious boy.

'In what strange machine are we travelling?' he asked, glancing around the inside of the car. 'Where are the wings?'

'D'you mean the car?'

'Car? Can't it lift up off the Earth?'

'No,' I replied, with a touch of wounded pride.

'And can't it move off this grey strip?' he enquired, pointing through the windscreen with his fingers, while I considered some of my own limitations.

'That strip is called the road,' I explained, thinking, where on Earth has this boy come from? 'And if we went off it at this speed, we'd be killed.'

'Are roads always so brutal? Who invented them?'

'Humans.'

Answering such simple questions was starting to feel oddly complicated. Who exactly was this boy, who radiated innocence and was shaking my inherited beliefs like an earthquake?

'Where have you come from? How did you get here?' I asked him, noticing something in his eyes that was strangely familiar.

'Are there many roads on the Earth?' he asked, without paying the slightest attention to what I'd said.

'Yes, any number of them.'

'I've been in a place without roads,' said the mysterious boy.

'But people would get lost there,' I pointed out, while my curiosity to know who he was and where he'd come from grew stronger and stronger.

'Where there are no roads on the Earth,' he continued, unfazed, 'don't people think of using the sky to orientate themselves?' And he looked up out of the window.

'At night,' I reflected, 'it's possible to navigate by the stars. But in very bright light, we'd risk going blind.'

'Ah!' the boy exclaimed. 'The blind see what no one dares to see. They must be the bravest people on this planet.'

I didn't know what to say in reply and a silence fell over us while the car carried on down its brutal grey strip.

Chapter Three

After a while, thinking he must have been too shy to answer, I decided to press him:

'What's happened? You can tell me. If you need something, I'll help you.'

But the boy said nothing.

'Go on, you can trust me. Tell me your name, and what the matter is,' I went on, not wanting to give up.

'What problem...?' he answered at last.

I tried to smooth things out a bit with a smile, so that he'd feel more comfortable. 'If you turn up like that, lying by the side of the road in the middle of nowhere, you've obviously got some sort of problem.'

After a moment's thought, he surprised me with a question: 'What exactly is a problem?'

I smiled, thinking he was being ironic.

'What is a problem?' he insisted, and I realized he was waiting for an answer.

Still surprised by his reaction, I thought that perhaps I hadn't understood the question.

'*Problema, problème...*' I tried it in a few other languages, even though it sounded more or less the same in all of them.

'I've heard the word,' he interrupted. 'But could you explain to me what it means?'

I racked my brains for the dictionary definition, but in vain, amazed that in a world positively overflowing with problems there might be a teenager who hadn't even come across the concept. Finally, after realizing I couldn't escape his penetrating gaze, I tried to put together an explanation of my own.

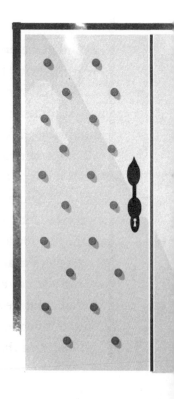

'A problem is like a door you haven't got the key to.'

'And what do you do when you come across a problem?' the boy wanted to know, becoming more and more interested in the conversation, even though he carried on staring into the distance.

'Well, the first thing to do is to see if the problem really is yours, if it's your path that it's blocking. That's vital,' I explained, 'because there are a lot of people who interfere in other people's problems, even though they haven't been asked for help. They lose time, waste their strength and prevent others from finding their own solutions.'

It was clear he agreed with this obvious truth, one which many adults don't accept. 'And if the problem really is yours?' he continued, turning towards me.

'Then you have to find the right key, and put it into the lock in the right sort of way.'

'It sounds simple,' the boy concluded with a nod.

'Don't you believe it,' I replied. 'Some people don't even find the key – and not for lack of imagination but because they're unwilling to try two or three times with the keys that they have, and sometimes they don't try at all. They want someone to hand them the key, or, even worse, to come and open the door for them.'

'And are they all capable of opening the door?'

'If you're convinced you can do it, then you al-most certainly can. But if you believe you can't, that practically guarantees you won't manage it.'

'And what happens to people who don't manage to open the door?' the boy pressed on.

'They have to try again and again until they do, or they'll never become what they could be.'

And then, as though thinking aloud, I added, 'There's no point losing our tempers, banging on the door and doing ourselves damage, blaming it for all our troubles. But now should we resign ourselves to living on this side of the door, dreaming of what might be on the other side?'

'And is there anything that justifies not opening that door?' he insisted, still not quite accepting my explanation.

'Far from it,' I exclaimed, 'although humans have developed a great capacity for justifying themselves. They blame their flaws on a lack of love or education, or on all the suffering they've had to deal with. They might eventually convince themselves that it's better not to cross the threshold, as it might be dangerous or threatening on the other side. Or they might cynically declare that they're not interested in what they might find if they walk through...But those are nothing more than ways of masking the pain of their failure. The longer we delay in confronting the obstacle in our path, the bigger the difficulties grow and the smaller we become; or, to put it another way, the longer we drag a problem with us, the heavier it becomes.'

I felt the boy's resistance lessening, but his persistent look, and the sadness and resignation on his face, made me go on. 'All this leads to unhappiness. The path to joy and spiritual fulfilment requires the courage to change and grow. We should always be ready to abandon the comfort of our position and face our problems again and again, until we're satisfied we've resolved them and can go through that door and make progress.'

'And what do I do to find the right key?' he went on, giving me no time to enjoy my neat analogy of the door, which he was clearly not ready to appreciate.

At that moment I had to lift my foot off the accelerator for a second as I'd caught up with a lorry full of livestock. When I looked at the petrol gauge, I was gripped by the sudden fear that we wouldn't have enough to get us to the next service station, which was miles away. I had to slow down in spite of myself so we would use less. Unfortunately my car wasn't fitted with one of those modern systems that shows you how many miles you can cover with the petrol you've got left. I reassured myself by thinking that the lorry would carry on behind me and could help if necessary, and so I greeted the driver with a broad smile as I overtook him, which he responded to with a friendly toot on his horn. Even today, seeing another human being in Patagonia is something to celebrate, which is why this friendly greeting has become a nice little custom.

'How do I find the right key?' insisted the boy, oblivious to my musings – and not giving up on the question now that he'd asked it.

'Just like that!' I replied, trying to hide the slight annoyance I was beginning to feel at the long journey. 'What I mean is, if you keep on asking your question over and over again, you'll always end up finding the answer. If you persevere and try all the keys you've got, eventually you'll open the door.'

And I thought, 'If you keep on with your questions for a few days, you'll end up driving me completely mad!' – which a voice inside me quietly corrected to 'completely sane'.

Chapter Four

Now that I'd encouraged him to keep asking things, nothing was going to stop the boy doing exactly that till the cows came home. But given that it was a long and dull journey, I decided that this strange conversation might become a pleasant distraction if, instead of thinking of the questions like an exam, I turned them into a sort of mind game. And, oddly enough, this change of perspective made my tiredness vanish as if by magic, and I found I was alert and ready to give my imagination free rein.

'You said that the key isn't enough on its own,' he continued, getting comfortable in his seat, 'that you also have to find the right way of using it. How do I find out what that way is?'

'Yes, that's right,' I began, with renewed energy, gesticulating as I spoke. 'The best way to solve a problem is not to think of it as a problem but just as a difficulty or a challenge. Technically, the obstacle is the same, but you'll be able to approach it with a positive attitude that sharpens the mind and beats a path towards more solutions in the future. You should be thankful to Providence that you come across the odd difficulty.'

'Be thankful for difficulties?' he asked in disbelief.

'Yes, because that will allow you to grow and to keep moving up the path to perfection. Like a wind that strengthens the roots of a tree so that the trunk is supported better. If you think of the obstacles you come across in this positive way, you'll waste less time complaining and lead a fuller life.'

When I saw that the boy was listening to me intently, I went straight on. 'Another thing you can do, once you've identified the difficulty, is look at it carefully, observe it from different angles, or even break it down into smaller difficulties.'

The boy nodded thoughtfully and said, 'I had to overcome an important difficulty by breaking it down into smaller ones.'

'What was that?' I asked with obvious curiosity.

'It would have been impossible for me to reach the Earth on my first attempt...' I made an effort to hide my astonishment and let him carry on. 'So I had to divide the journey up and make seven stops on other asteroids.'

I decided that, even though he seemed to have lost his marbles, my companion had an extraordinary imagination.

After a silence in which he seemed lost in thought, he added, 'On one journey I met someone who had a problem that couldn't be solved.'

'Oh, really?' I said distractedly.

'It was a man who drank to forget.'

'To forget what?' I asked lazily.

'That he was full of shame and guilt.'

'Why?' I wanted to know.

'Because he drank,' the boy replied, coming full circle with this story that was confusing him so much.

'Feelings of guilt,' I remarked, 'paralyse us and keep us from solving a lot of problems. Taking responsibility makes those feelings dis-

32

appear and allows us to do more positive things, such as making up as far as possible for the harm we've done. Or simply moving on and not falling back into the behaviour that made us feel guilty in the first place.'

'But if you've done something bad,' he queried, 'how can you avoid guilt?'

'Guilt didn't help that man who was driven to drink. It's a useless punishment that will rob him of his energy and that he's persevering with because he's stopped loving himself. Didn't you ask him why he'd started drinking in the first place?'

'No…' answered the boy, hesitating, and I afforded at least a little smile, as it felt like it would have been harder to find an unknown pharaoh's tomb than ask a question the boy hadn't yet asked himself.

'Loneliness, lack of love, some frustration or other…I don't know the original reason, but without a doubt being addicted to drink was nothing more than a consequence. Right there, you have a poignant example of the destructive effects you get from not overcoming difficulties.'

'How naive I was to judge him as I did!' the boy decided wretchedly. 'Perhaps my affection would have been the key to open the door that he couldn't walk through.'

'Our lives would be a lot better,' I added, 'if we

stopped judging ourselves and others – if, rather than complaining about all kinds of disadvantages and torturing ourselves with questions of whether or not we deserved our difficulties, or if we could have avoided them, we applied our abilities instead to solving those problems and accepting what we can't change. As an old oriental proverb says: better to light a match than to keep cursing the darkness.'

The boy was listening to me with interest, so I decided to keep thinking aloud.

'Sometimes you'll discover that, when you change your point of view, the obstacle disappears because often the only difficulty is in us – and it's nothing but our rigid, short-sighted way of seeing things.'

'The difficulty is in us?' he repeated incredulously, as he looked down towards his belly button.

'Most of the time, yes,' I replied. 'But the solution is too. The world of ideas and emotions drags the material world after it. However you imagine things to be, that's probably how they'll go for you. Up to a certain point, you create the reality around you, as though you were a little god over your surroundings.'

'How is that possible? Is reality on this planet not one and the same for all men?' asked the boy, surprised.

'Perhaps the total reality itself is one and the same,'

I mused, 'but we can only perceive as much of it as our consciousness has evolved to perceive, according to the strength of our senses. When we sift out of that total reality a few ideas, facts and people that we agree or disagree with, in truth all we're doing is reflecting our own image.'

'Do you mean that people never actually come face-to-face with reality, but only with themselves reflected through that reality?'

'That becomes pretty obvious when you look at just how limited our senses are, and that's proved by machines that can capture sound waves at frequen-

cies so high or so low that our ears can't pick them up, or microscopes and telescopes that multiply our field of vision. But we don't always understand as clearly that observing our own environment and the things that happen to us is one of the best ways of getting to know ourselves, because everything in the outside world that affects us demonstrates that we aren't in harmony with the corresponding principle inside us.'

'Why do you say things in such a complicated way?' he complained.

'It's as though a person's miserliness could only bother someone else who was a miser, because a generous person would consider it a simple fact, without letting it affect them too much,' I proposed, seeing that my travelling companion was starting to understand. 'In the same way, everyone who fights with their bad neighbours or relatives – or against the injustices inflicted on them by their bosses, against society or any number of other things – whether or not they're right, are in fact fighting with themselves,' I concluded, rounding off my idea.

'Who could win a fencing match against a mirror?' asked the boy, amazed.

'The problem with those people is they don't understand that anything that's in conflict with its environment is doomed to failure,' I said. 'Most human suffering comes from resistance to the circumstances that surround us, and from friction between human beings and the laws of nature. The wise man is in harmony with everything that exists. He contemplates reality and realizes that everything that exists, whether he likes it or not, is how it ought to be. He also knows that before we improve anything in the world, there is a lot we need to improve in ourselves.'

'Is everything that exists good simply because it exists? Why do you always make things so complicated? Please give me an example I can understand,' implored my young companion.

'When you push hard against a wall,' I began, 'you can feel the wall resisting with the same force. If you push harder, the wall will resist harder, too. The solution lies in taking your hands off the wall: the resistance will disappear by itself. The person who recognizes the wall's right to exist doesn't need to push it any more, and isn't affected by its existence either.'

'That's all very well,' he conceded, 'but if it's true that we only know part of reality, then each person lives in his own world, and there are as many worlds as there are people.'

'Maybe it would be easier for you to imagine it as

the pieces of a jigsaw puzzle that, all together, make up a greater reality than any of them does on its own. The most amazing thing is that each person is capable of changing and transforming the world as far as their own perceptions go, without fighting and without the intervention of external forces –'

'I understand what you mean now,' he

interrupted. 'If I see a face I don't like in the mirror, the only thing I can do is smile.'

'Exactly,' I agreed. 'And in the same way, if you

have an aggressive neighbour, try to be kinder yourself. If you want a good son, start by being a good father, or vice versa. And the same goes for husbands, wives, bosses, employees...Really, there's only one way of changing the world, and that's by changing yourself.'

Chapter Five

We were both quiet for a while then, contemplating the immensity of the Patagonian landscape. An incessant wind blew across that barren wasteland with barely a moment of respite, biting at the sawn-off cones of the mountains. In the distance, on a hillside dotted with vegetation, red streaks of firebush marked the path into the valley.

'Perhaps this whole universe was created in the image and likeness of a supreme being who wanted to know himself, to experience himself.'

The thought didn't seem to surprise the boy, who immediately asked, 'If that were true, what should people on this planet do? Are they free? Or are they tied to the road, like you?'

41

'The way I see it,' I replied, 'to live is to learn. The more our consciousnesses develop, the more easily we can distil the inherent meaning out of the things that happen to us. Sometimes the pains and illnesses we reject are the ones that could bring us the greatest spiritual riches. That's why, whatever cards you're dealt, you should be grateful for a life that gives you the opportunity to evolve. Fate always finds a way to make us learn the things we resist the most, the things we least want to accept.'

'What is fate? It sounds like a strict master...' the boy reflected.

'It's the path each person follows.'

'Is it possible to change it?' he asked with growing confusion.

'Yes,' I replied laconically, thinking of all the libraries of the world, overflowing with tomes in which people have tried to find a definitive answer to that question.

As the boy was still giving me a perplexed look, I decided to resort to an image. 'Imagine yourself as a river that has to flow for ever. You decide to dodge the mountains and try to find the easiest path to the sea.

Difficulties,' I continued, 'are like the rocks you'll find on the way. If you drag them with you, they'll end up forming a dam that will slow you down. But if you overcome them one by one as they appear, your current will be constant and your waters clear, as though the contact with each stone increases your brilliance. At some point you might feel guilty and unworthy of that transparency, and then you'll look for a way to muddy your waters. Perhaps you'll become lazy and stray on to level ground, until you come to a stop on some plain. Or you might become rash and tumble down a steep slope, and form a waterfall; or you might wander into winding gullies and become lost. Perhaps your soul will harden like ice, or your cool caress might be burned up in the mirages of the desert...'

'If I were a river, I wouldn't like to freeze or burn up in the desert,' he admitted.

'In that case, develop purity and you will be transparent; imagine yourself as generous and you'll fertilize your surroundings; rejuvenate yourself and your coolness will quench the thirst of the places you pass. Trust in your ideals and you will inspire others; become aware of your being and you will awaken those who live in their sleep. Live with purpose and you will fulfil your destiny.'

I stopped talking. Our gazes drifted out over those wild plains, climbing slowly towards the bluish ghosts of the mountains.

Chapter Six

The boy seemed delighted with the image of the river and was absorbed in his thoughts for a while.

I soon realized that for some hours now I'd been driving with a stranger at my side (a friendly stranger, perhaps, but a stranger all the same), not knowing the slightest thing about him. Although I wanted to get to know this singular young man, my intuition told me that revelations would arrive by themselves, and all the quicker if I didn't try to force them. Sometimes people are like oysters: the only thing we need to do is wait for them to release the pearl that they've been harbouring inside.

But not even a master in the esoteric art of the unpredictable could have anticipated the next question.

'What about sheep, do they have problems, too?'

'What's that?'

'Do sheep have problems, too?' the boy repeated patiently, as though I were one of those people who need to be told things twice to understand them.

I thanked God that we were short on petrol and

had had to slow down, because a question like that could have thrown us off the road. A single look at him was enough to know that he was perfectly serious. I was disconcerted, and answered frankly. 'In all honesty, I don't know. I suppose you'd have to be a sheep to be sure, don't you think?'

To my surprise, the boy nodded and seemed quite satisfied, if not by the logic of my question then at least to be spending his time with an adult capable of acknowledging his own ignorance. Then he added,

'So what you're saying is that to know the problems of a flower you'd have to be a flower. Is that it?'

But I wasn't prepared to spend the whole afternoon on the defensive, waiting for the next surprise from my opponent. It was a perfect opportunity to launch a sharp counter-attack.

'That's where you're wrong, my friend,' I parried, preparing my first move. 'You don't have to be a flower to know that a flower has problems: they're too beautiful and defenceless. Some of them have thorns to protect them from people who are lured by their beauty and want to cut them from the plant and put them in a vase.'

He looked at me, horrified. I thought he was going to faint, but he composed himself and managed to say, 'And do the thorns keep them safe?'

His face seemed to beg for an affirmative answer, but, puffed up by my tyrannical over-statement of the truth, I pressed on regardless. This was nothing more than a game, after all.

'No,' I replied. 'The thorns don't keep them safe. That's their problem.'

The expression on his face told me that, for my eccentric companion, this was no game. Later, I would discover with much sadness that it was a question of life and death concerning a very close friend of his.

Sometimes, without realizing it, we adults play with children's deepest feelings, and destroy things much more valuable than anything they can break by themselves.

It would have been useless to point out to him that flowers have survived for thousands of years with that problem, and even that their nature is capable of withstanding it. That wasn't what worried the boy. What he wanted was to save one particular, unique flower; and when a flower is unique, there is no statistic or botanical book in the world that will bring comfort.

As if he were thinking aloud, he added, 'Perhaps

if they gave up their beauty, if they hid themselves away, they wouldn't have problems...but then they wouldn't be flowers either. They need our admiration to be happy. Vanity, that's their problem,' he concluded.

At that moment the sad expression I'd seen before, briefly kept away by curiosity, returned to his eyes.

'Well, anyway, I don't care about the problems of sheep and flowers.' Only later would I understand what he was referring to. 'I'm looking for someone I haven't seen in a while. He's a bit like you, but his machine flies.'

'A plane?' I asked, rather confused.

'Yes, that's it, a plane.'

'And where does he live?' I asked, hoping I could help him, as there were a few aviation clubs in the region that I'd seen on the map.

'I don't know,' he answered sadly. And then he reflected, 'I didn't know people lived so far away from one another.' Seeing I was perplexed, he clarified: 'The Earth is very big, you see. And my planet is very small.'

'How do you plan on finding him?' I asked, while I woke up the part of my brain where the large number of detective novels I'd read as a teenager were stored. But his reply would have foxed Poirot himself.

'He gave me stars that laugh,' he said nostalgically. For a moment his feelings overwhelmed him, and I saw his eyes misting up.

It was at that moment, as I tried to imagine the figure of the aviator at whom the stars smiled, that I realized who my companion was.

Of course! The sheep, the flower, the blue cape...I should have recognized him from the start, but I was too wrapped up in the world of my own obscure asteroid.

Chapter Seven

At that same moment, as though coming to our rescue just as the car's motor sucked up the last few gallons left in the tank, a petrol station appeared before our eyes. I breathed a sigh of relief. After filling the tank and checking the oil and water levels, I had to insist that the Young Prince go and freshen up in the bathroom.

When we'd been on the road again for a while, I asked him, 'He's the one who gave you the sheep, isn't he?'

We both knew who I was referring to, but I felt the pain in his expression when he replied, 'That's what I used to think...'

'What do you mean?' I asked, encouraging him to go on. Sadness, disbelief, anger and then sadness again all flitted over his face in rapid succession. In their depths those eyes seemed to be burning, perhaps with hope. My intuition was telling me that it was hope that had brought him here.

When he finally spoke, it was with the muted sound of resignation. 'It's a sad story. I don't think you'd be interested,' he said, without wondering for a moment how I knew about his sheep.

'Of course I'm interested!' My answer was so enthusiastic I was afraid I'd have to explain why I was so interested in a sheep I'd never seen.

To my relief the Young Prince started to tell his tale; it was as though my opponent had overlooked the move that would have put me in checkmate.

One morning, when the Young Prince was busy with his daily chores of cleaning his planet and putting everything in order ('It's important to keep the planet nice and clean, you know,' he pointed out), a tuft of grass that he was just about to pull up said to him, 'If you pull me up, you'll be making another mistake.'

'What d'you mean, "another mistake"?' he asked, fearing it might be a trap.

'I mean that you'll be depriving yourself of a pretty intelligent tuft of grass that could be a lot of use to you. And after all, what harm could I do? I'm in your hands. You can pull me up whenever you like, but I think you're going to need me. You will be my master and I your servant.'

Before making a decision, the Young Prince asked again, 'What did you mean by "another mistake"? What was the first?'

'A very simple one, master. You think there's a sheep in that box, don't you?'

'But of course there's a sheep in the box!' cried the Young Prince indignantly. 'It's a lovely white sheep that my friend from Earth gave me. He forgot to give me the strap and the post though, because of the pain my leaving caused him. That's why I can't let him out to pasture: he might run off and eat the flower.'

He stopped to get his breath back, and when he was ready to pull the grass out of the ground, she spoke to him again. 'Master, if you let me explain my-self instead of being swept away by your emotions, I think I can clear up the whole matter for you.' And the grass opened out one of her blades, on which, to the Young Prince's astonishment, a detailed picture appeared of a sheep next to a boy.

After looking at it for a moment, he had to admit that he'd never seen such an accurate drawing.

'It isn't a drawing, it's a photograph,' the tuft of grass pointed out a touch triumphantly, feeling she'd prolonged her life a little. And she went on, 'This is an image that captures reality exactly as it is. As you can see, a sheep comes up above a child's waist. If you had asked me, I could have told you that even newborn lambs are bigger than your eight-inch box.'

Then, adopting a more compassionate tone, the grass pushed the knife home. 'Master, I'm sorry to have to tell you this, but as your servant I must warn you about this so-called friend, who has abused your trust, because the box is, in fact, empty.'

At that moment, the world of the Young Prince collapsed all around him. It was the saddest day of his life. Afterwards he was never sure of anything or anyone again. No sunset would console him now.

Chapter Eight

I saw tears running down his cheeks as he spoke, and I had to make an effort to keep my eyes on the strip of asphalt rising out of the grey haze, growing darker now and stretching to the horizon.

'Then the tuft of grass started explaining things to me that I hadn't understood before. She warned me about the malicious tricks of flowers and the treacherous behaviour of men. I was initiated into the chemical and physical sciences and instructed in the most up-to-date statistical and economic variables. I learned dozens of virtual games on one of her blades that lit up like a multicoloured screen. But without my sheep, the days grew longer and the evenings grew sadder.'

One night, the Young Prince had a realistic and

deeply affecting dream. He was sitting next to his friend in the cockpit of a plane, flying over the Earth's gorgeous landscapes. There were majestic mountains with beautiful valleys between them, where crystal-clear rivers reflected every now and then the shadow of the plane. He could make out meadows in flower, like braided rugs, sheltered from the wind by dense woods. As they were flying at a low altitude, they could see deer, horses, goats, hares and foxes running freely over the fields, and even trout leaping joyfully in the streams. The Young Prince had no questions to ask and his friend had no explanations to give him.

They did nothing more than look at the marvels before them and smile, although they sometimes pointed things out to one another and laughed, too. He had never felt so happy. Suddenly his friend started to turn around and gestured that he was going to land on a grass-covered hill. The landing was perfect, as though the Earth had softened its surface to give them a loving welcome. As soon as they had got out of the plane, the aviator took him to the opposite slope of the hill, where a large flock of white sheep and their little lambs were grazing peacefully, and said to him, 'They are all for you. I don't know how many there are; it didn't seem important to count

them. I started raising them the very day you left, and the flock has grown along with my affection for you.'

The Young Prince was moved, and as he went towards his friend to embrace him, he woke up alone on his dark and silent planet. His sweet tears turned bitter as they fell, and he thought he heard a voice inside him saying, 'Look for your friend and let him explain his reasons to you. Only then will you see the stars again...'

Very early the next day, he went to say goodbye to his flower, which he'd grown a little distant from of late. She was pale and withered, as though the boy's lack of attention had made her waste away.

'I'm going. Goodbye,' the Young Prince announced, but the flower didn't respond.

He stroked her, covering her with his hands, but still she didn't move. There was nothing keeping him there now.

A few dangerous shoots of baobab were sprouting up one side of the path and the earth was starting to shake, doubtless because the volcanoes hadn't been cleaned. But none of that was important now. He was getting ready to set off when he came across the tuft of grass.

'Where are you off to so early?' she asked.

The Young Prince said nothing, so as not to alarm her, but his eyes told the grass what she wanted to know.

'You can't go! You're my master!' she cried.

'But I'm setting you free,' he answered.

'You can't do this to me. You know that I can't live with freedom. I need someone to serve and you need someone to serve you,' the grass insisted.

'If I couldn't live without you, I would be the slave and you would be my mistress,' the Young Prince pointed out.

'I'll die if you leave me here. There's no other master who can pull the weeds up and soon they'll cover the whole planet,' she implored.

The Young Prince hesitated for a moment, but the decision was already made. He would follow the voice from his dream.

'If you want to come with me, I'll have to pull you out of the ground,' he said, as he grabbed her firmly by the stalks.

'No, no!' shouted the grass.

'Goodbye, then,' he said, and set off.

'That's how my journey started,' the Young Prince went on, and I realised that his journey had been a very long one. 'Finally I arrived on the Earth, in that very solitary place. The animals and flowers don't speak to me now like they did when I was a child. I didn't find a single human being who could tell me where I was. Exhausted and not knowing where to go, I collapsed asleep just where you found me...'

He fell quiet, and I understood that, sooner or later, all of us have to go on an arduous journey into the depths of our being. And no conquest can offer us a greater reward.

Chapter Nine

'As you can see, it's a very sad story, and I don't think there's much you can do to help me,' concluded the Young Prince. I was so absorbed in his account that, when he finished, I had the feeling the car had been guided by another hand.

'It really is a sad story,' I agreed. 'But you're wrong when you say I can't help you. There are lots of things I could do!'

This immediately put the Young Prince on the defensive. 'But don't you see? I've lost a friend who made the stars smile. I've lost the sheep that kept me company in the evenings and the flower that brought joy to my life with her games and her beauty. Don't you understand that I'll never see the tuft of grass that was my protector and my adviser again, nor my

little planet, which might explode from all the volcanic eruptions? And you think you can help me?' he asked defiantly. This burst of passion had brought some of the colour back to his cheeks.

'Actually, yes,' I answered steadily. 'I can help you to get back everything you've lost and more because, in fact, what you've lost is your joy in life, happiness itself…But I can only do it if you'll let me, and if you're ready to help yourself.'

He gave me a sceptical look but said nothing, so I continued. 'This is the first serious difficulty you've come across in your life, and you need to resolve it. And the truth is that, even though you feel overwhelmed by it now, it isn't the end of the world. You've got the wish to overcome the situation on your side, which is something that both your spiritual nature and your animal instinct command you to do in any case.'

'How can you be so sure that I have the strength to solve the problem, when I don't feel like I do myself?'

'Good point,' I noted, congratulating myself on having got his attention. 'I'll tell you why I'm so sure.

First of all, you had the courage to abandon the apparent safety of your planet and go out into the universe in search of a solution. Secondly, in spite of feeling exhausted, you managed to end up somewhere you'd get help. If you'd let yourself land right on the road or in the middle of some field, you'd probably be dead by now. And thirdly, in our first conversation we talked about obstacles, problems, which means you're already trying to find useful information for getting out of the deadlock you're in.'

When I saw that I was gaining his attention and confidence, I pressed on. 'We talked before about how to solve problems. If you like, we can look at the difficulty you're in right now. And I say "difficulty" because I know you can overcome it, and even though you don't believe it, the key is in you.'

His reaction was instant. 'How can you say that? My life was peaceful and happy until I discovered that my friend had deceived me. That and nothing else is the cause of my troubles,' retorted the indignant Young Prince.

'You're putting the problem outside yourself and blaming someone else for your situation, which is an excellent way of not resolving it,' I said calmly, while his eyes seemed to burn through me. Before he could say anything, I picked up my thread. 'I'll show you in a minute, my young friend, that this supposed deception was no deception, at least not one committed with the negative intention you're assuming. But let's suppose for the moment that your friend did trick you. That would justify being annoyed with him, feeling disillusioned and even sad, but not the fact that you no longer admire your flower's beauty, or the poetry of the sunsets or the music of the stars.'

I had my passenger's full attention now, so I spoke a little more gently. 'Your friend's apparent deceit had a devastating effect on your life because your life's foundations were too fragile. I can well imagine that your sheep couldn't cheer you up any more, and that the flower, in all her self-absorption, was no comfort. It's obvious that your daily business wasn't fulfilling you spiritually, and that you hadn't cultivated any work, any craftsmanship that might have served as a temporary refuge. Perhaps your whole reality had become flat and the only thing that sustained the tranquillity of your days was yearning for your absent friend. And so it makes sense that when that single support collapsed, everything else fell down with it. In fact, your world was already empty, like the flower that had withered before you left. Your friend's supposed deceit was no more than the trigger, and certainly not the real cause of your present situation. The sooner you accept that, the quicker you'll be able to move towards a solution.'

It looked like defensiveness and acceptance were battling it out inside him. I hastened to add another observation that to me seemed obvious. 'If you had been more secure, if you had had more confidence in your feelings, the grass wouldn't have found her way so easily into the crack that had opened up in your heart, and she wouldn't have had such a destructive influence on your life.'

The Young Prince made to protest, perhaps to stand up for the grass, but using the last air in my lungs I carried straight on. 'Why do we so often prefer the person who disabuses us to the one who has given us the gift of an illusion?'

My question threw him momentarily, which gave me the pause I needed to go on. 'Beware those who destroy your dreams with the excuse of doing you a favour, because they generally don't have anything good to replace them with!'

And I asked myself if there wasn't a little wisdom in the ancient custom of executing the bringer of bad news. Over the years I have discovered that, most of the time, the news has been wrong, or the messenger's intention has not been what he made out; or that, where there was nothing I could do, I would have preferred to hear the news as late as possible.

I carried on with my little speech. 'Sooner or later, dreams stop being dreams. We even wake up from the dream of life, with death; or perhaps it's the other way round. I can tell you with certainty that your friend gave you the loveliest sheep in the world – the one that you imagined in your fantasy, the only one you could look after and that could go with you to your little planet. Didn't you enjoy his company as you watched the sunsets? Didn't you go to him in the night so that he wouldn't feel alone, and so that you too wouldn't feel so alone? Didn't you think that he belonged to you because you had tamed him, and that you belonged to him? There's no doubt that he was more real, more alive, than the one you saw in the photograph, because that one was just a sheep, whereas the one inside the box was your sheep.' At that moment I understood why, when I travel, I don't take photos of my loved

ones with me: the pictures I have of them in my heart are more vivid.

Then I stopped talking because, when I turned for a moment towards my young companion, I realized that his eyes were filling with tears, as though he had wanted to cry for a long time.

'Thank you,' said the Young Prince, and, reaching towards me for a hug, he laid his head on my shoulder. Slowly, he drifted off to sleep.

Chapter Ten

A few hours later, as night was falling, we were approaching the place where I had planned to spend the night. The road was as deserted as it had been during the day, but there were a few signs of habitation: white poplars lined the road here and there, and sheltered a garden from the wind; a handful of isolated huts stood next to a huge sheepfold.

In contrast to the rapid nightfall on the planet of the Young Prince, Patagonian dusks are long and silent, and as they advance, half the sky is washed in a glorious array of pinkish, lilac and purple hues. That afternoon the sunset was so exquisite that I felt I should wake up the Young Prince so he could see it.

'Look how beautiful it is!' I told him, pointing to the

horizon, and taking my eyes off the road for a second as I did so.

'Watch out!' the boy warned me, but it was too late.

There was a sharp impact against the front of the vehicle and the car gave a jolt. As I hit the brakes, I could see in the rear-view mirror a white animal, presumably a sheep, lying on the tarmac. I stopped, got out and went to the front of the car to see what the damage was. The Young Prince looked at me as if I didn't know what I was doing, and went off in the opposite direction.

When I realized he was going to help the injured animal, I said to him, 'Don't bother. After an impact like that, it'll be dead. There won't be anything we can do.'

But the boy, who had started running towards the white shape, shouted, 'Today you taught me that there is always something we can do, even if we don't believe it ourselves!'

His words rang in my ears as I bent down to check that the only visible damage was a dent in the bumper. The Young Prince had managed to show me, if only for a moment, that my heart was as hard as that strip of metal which, cold as it might have been, had at least had the decency to yield to the blow.

Feeling a little guilty after my rebuke from the boy, I walked towards him. As I approached, I saw an enormous white dog with its head lying in the boy's lap, which he was holding and stroking. Despite the moans of the dying animal, it was a scene of real tenderness.

I looked up and saw a thickset man making his way over to us from a nearby hut, his face darkened and threatening. I realized he must be the dog's owner. I thought it would be prudent to leave and avoid a pointless argument, and told my young friend that we had better be off. But he didn't move, and carried on stroking the terrified animal, which by all accounts seemed to be dying. The man was still coming towards us, and so, sensing danger, I thought it would be best to offer him some compensation. When he had reached us I took out my wallet and mumbled some words of apology, but he gestured with disgust that I shouldn't move, and for a few painful minutes the three of us were silent.

The image of that dog is still engraved in my memory today. My new friend had been right. Of course there was something we could do. As the Young Prince looked lovingly into his eyes, the enormous white dog became less afraid, because he didn't feel so alone. I had the feeling that this rural man felt the change too. Eventually, the dog, with an almost human look, seemed to be thanking the boy. First his left eye closed, then his right. Then his whole body gave a shudder, just once, and he stopped moving.

The Young Prince stroked him for a few more minutes. When it was clear that all life had left the dog, the boy turned to look at the man for the first time, his eyes brimming with tears. The man, with unexpected tenderness, placed a weathered hand on the boy's golden hair, and after lifting the dead dog carefully, gathered it up in his arms.

'Come with me,' he said to the boy. When I made a movement to follow them, he stopped me, saying, 'No, not you. Just him.' And then, to reassure me, he added, 'Don't worry. There are things you can't put a price on.'

Chapter Eleven

It's impossible to describe the feelings I was overcome with at that moment. I felt aggrieved and misunderstood – after all, my reaction had been the usual one in the unthinking society we live in. In fact, most people wouldn't have stopped at all, or if they had, instead of offering an apology and some financial compensation as I did, they would have reprimanded the animal's owner for letting him run loose and pose a danger to drivers. I also worried about what might happen to the boy, as though being in the company of another human was more dangerous than leaving him abandoned by the side of the road where I'd found him that same day. I reflected that we often act out of fear and mistrust, instead of letting ourselves be led by a love that we mostly repress. Humanity has the curse (or blessing) that all human beings are interconnected. As long as any one of them is suffering, none of them will be completely happy. Nothing in the world is unknown to us, neither its pain nor its joy, because ours is a world that still suffers even though there is bliss, which is still joyful even though there is pain. The more we know our suffering, the more we will enjoy our happiness. And so share what you feel, be it song or scar. Don't be a stranger!

As the sun sank majestically into the dark, there was a new dawn rising in my heart.

Suddenly I saw the Young Prince coming back alone, walking as though he had something in his arms. As he came up to me, I could see that it was an adorable white puppy. I could scarcely believe it: the man from whom we had just snatched the life of a beloved companion was giving us a new life as a gift.

It was a miracle of love, and the first lesson I learned from the Young Prince. I had shared my experience with him in words, and he, like a true master, was showing me wisdom in silence. At that moment it was clearer to me than ever that a thousand books on the art of loving add nothing to a simple kiss, nor a thousand speeches on love to a single affectionate gesture.

'It's a Kuvasz puppy,' he said. 'Did you know?'

'Yes,' I replied, 'they come from Tibet, and today there are also some in parts of Eastern Europe.'

'The man thought I'd look after him well,' he explained to me, still stroking and gazing at his new friend. 'I will call him Wings, in memory of my aviator friend, because he is as white and fluffy as the clouds.'

The boy's voice had taken on a new sweetness that I hadn't noticed in him before. And so the three of us, feeling comforted, got into the car and set off again towards the little hotel where we would spend the night. The Young Prince started to regain his natural cheerfulness with amazing speed.

After we had eaten supper, we got them to let Wings sleep in our room with us. The puppy only calmed down when my young friend took him up on to the bed and hugged him to his chest. Soon the two of them were asleep. A little smile crept on to the Young Prince's face. I knew that as he flew up into his dreams, Wings would be going with him.

Chapter Twelve

The next morning we hit the road again early, amazed at the vast expanse opening up before us. Even though it was arid, it was still lovely to behold – perhaps because deep inside ourselves we were open to its beauty. The Young Prince had Wings curled up in his lap, and was stroking him distractedly. I could see something was worrying him, but I respected his silence.

After a while, he finally said, 'I don't want to be a serious person.'

'That's good,' I replied.

'But I need to grow up,' he continued.

'That's true,' I agreed.

'So how do I grow up without becoming a serious

person?' the Young Prince asked, revealing what was on his mind.

'That's another good question,' I replied. 'So good, in fact, that I've never found a decent answer. When we're young we go out into the world and find it's very different from the one we got to know through our parents – at least those of us lucky enough, who were read fairy tales about people with magic powers, stories of princes and princesses in enchanted castles. And at that moment, we come up against selfishness, incomprehension, aggression and deceit. We try to defend ourselves and hold on to our innocence, but injustice, violence, shallowness and lack of love torment us. And then, instead of spreading light and joy around it, our spirit starts to tremble in the face of reality's painful but unstoppable advance. Some end up abandoning their treasured dreams, and root themselves in the false security of rational thought. They become serious people, and they adore numbers and routines as those give them a sense of security. But because nothing is ever entirely secure, they are never quite happy. They start amassing possessions because they are always lacking something. "Having" doesn't make them happy – because it stops them from "being". They look so hard at the means that they forget about the end.'

'So if it doesn't make them happy, why do adults devote most of their lives to having more and more things?' asked the Young Prince, quite logically.

'Thinking that happiness depends on piling up possessions is a reassuring self-deception. As more importance is given to having and not having, the search is aimed at something that lies outside of us, which allows us to avoid having to look inside ourselves. According to that rationale, we can be happy without changing, just by getting this or that.'

'And people don't realize?' the Young Prince wanted to know, resisting the conclusion that people could be so blind.

'What has happened, my young friend, is that our society has invented so many things for us to own that people don't realize they've gone down the wrong road until they fail to get that last thing. You've already seen how they'll cling to the slightest support, however small, before admitting that they're wrong and need to change. The problem is that by the time they get that last thing, they've lost some of the initial, fundamental things. They're like those jugglers who keep seven hats in the air at once. And just think: they're only doing it with seven! What's more, as soon as people get close to the thing they were after, they only know what it is they want next. So what they thought was their final goal isn't that after all, and they fritter their lives away on a useless search, jumping from one thing to the next as though all those objects were so many stepping stones in a river they'll never finish crossing. On the whole, people who are always going after more get trapped in the future. They never live in the present, never enjoy it, because their attention is always focused on something that's yet to happen.'

'And what should they do instead?' asked my young friend, stroking Wings, who was still dozing in his lap.

'Nothing but dive head first into the reality of being, and let themselves be carried along by it. They should concentrate on living, being and loving in every moment, and not get so obsessed with their final destination. When obstacles come up, they could adopt new forms of being which would reaffirm their essential qualities, like a river whose depth and direction are always changing. The most important thing is to be as attentive and aware as possible, with our senses awakened and our ability to love utterly intact, so that we can exist right here and right now, and enjoy life and be creative, trapped in neither the past nor the future.'

'So should we give up all our memories?' the Young Prince suddenly cut in, I suppose because the memories of his flower and his friend were very important to him.

'No. All the good memories and gratifying experiences you carry with you can be of comfort in difficult moments, or when you feel alone. What you should avoid is clinging to that past, that secure place, because you could end up trapped in it and stop yourself from living your experiences in the present. The past is secure because it's closed, dead. Despite that, some still prefer the peace and security of death to the uncertainty of life, with all its possibilities for joy and suffering.'

A moment later, I added, 'Another way that memories conspire against your happiness is in making you want to feel things you have felt in the past, that will never happen. Just as the water in a river is never the same, situations in life are never repeated in exactly the same way. Despite that, it's amazing to see how many people get trapped trying to relive the same experiences. It stops them enjoying new ones that might be just as good or better. This is where a person is just like an animal that goes back again and again to a place where it once found food, until it dies of hunger simply because it never explored a little further afield.'

For a long while, the two of us were lost in our thoughts, with nothing to interrupt them, as that landscape is graceful enough to remain respectfully in the background.

When the Young Prince finally spoke, he took me by surprise.

'Thank you,' he said.

'Why are you thanking me?' I asked.

'For saving me from unhappiness,' he replied.

'What do you mean?' I wanted to know.

'Well, I've been thinking about what you said and I've discovered I had a thought deeply rooted in my mind: I would never be truly happy again until I found another friend like the aviator I miss so much. However, that thought contains all three obstacles to happiness that you mentioned before. First of all, the need for "someone like him" that would stop me from considering other people, different from him but perhaps just as interesting and noble. Secondly, the question of "security", because I'd never be totally secure in the thought that I'd found someone identical to him. And thirdly, "the search", which would make me focus on the future, on someone I might yet meet, and not value the people already around me.'

'I can see that you've understood me perfectly,' I conceded, with the pride of a master who has found his best pupil.

'You can never be attentive enough,' said the Young Prince.

'No, never,' I repeated, and we both smiled.

In the silence that followed, I could tell there was something lingering in his expression that tied him to the past, but I decided to wait before I was sure.

While the car carried on calmly devouring the road as though it were one endless grey string of spaghetti, my anxiousness to arrive fell away – because I was starting to enjoy every moment of that journey.

Chapter Thirteen

As it was almost time to eat, and because I feared Wings would lay a princely gift in my friend's lap, I decided to stop at a restaurant with a few vehicles parked outside that appeared suddenly at the side of the road. As we went in I noticed, at a table where a family was eating, five pairs of young eyes staring in astonishment at the Young Prince's outfit. I quickly steered us towards a table that was right over on the other side of the room, but even that didn't end the hullabaloo, which was as loud as if one of the three wise men had come in without his camel.

I realized the children's reaction was getting to my friend, who sat down with his back to them. Their father's efforts to calm them down, waving around the chicken leg he was holding, weren't exactly fruitful, given that he too was trying to solve the mystery of our quaint appearance. The mother, who was sitting with her back to us, carried on eating without paying the slightest attention, as though a sort of selective deafness allowed her to shut herself off every now and then from the uproar those rascals were mounting. Everything I said during the meal was aimed at bolstering my friend's self-esteem, which was a little bruised by this reaction to the trivial matter of clothing. I spoke to him about the importance of differences and variety, the things that enrich a group.

'If we couldn't tell flowers apart by their scent, their shape or their colour, we would never stop to look at any one in particular. Differences,' I added, 'are the first things that attract us, and when we admire that flower, we make it unique.'

Privately, I was lamenting the fact that those same things that interest us and complement us are also used to separate and divide us. As we tucked into a dish of succulent grilled meat with potatoes and salad, I remarked that many of the geniuses of history had suffered the rejection of their contemporaries, even though humanity would not have evolved if those people had not held fast to their beliefs. I attacked the mediocrity of those who, the moment they see a spark of creativity being lit, rush to put it out like a troop of firemen, instead of letting the air feed its transformative fire.

'My dear friend,' I said to him, placing a hand on his shoulder, 'you have to forgive people for their first reaction being to judge appearances. But if you're sure of yourself and keep faith in the values that guide you, they will accept you in the end, even if it's just to show off to their circle of friends that they know someone as special as you.'

Then, leaning back in my chair, I said, 'Of course there's a much simpler, easier way of relating to people...'

'And what's that?' the Young Prince wanted to know, a little more interested now.

'Doing just the opposite. Instead of getting their attention with your external appearance and trying to show them how you are inside, you can choose to blend in with them, try and look like them, and then mark yourself out as someone unique and special on the strength of your values alone,' I explained.

'What would you do?' he asked, looking at me intently.

I thought about it for a while before answering. 'If you choose the first option, people will either get close to you or keep their distance, and build up positive or negative prejudices, without really getting to know you, basing it all on your appearance. The good side to that is that you'll get lots of people's attention; the drawback is, some of them will distance themselves from you for good. While the second option will mean you won't stand out, and a lot of people won't even know you exist – or they'll only find out later. If I had to choose, I'd take the second one. It's slower and more discreet, but more profound too. Either way, the important thing is that you don't stop being yourself in order to fit with what other people want.'

'Wouldn't you worry that your message would be lost and that a lot of people would never even know you'd passed through this world?' asked the boy.

I realized he was trying not to show how afraid he was of never finding the person he was looking for. I remember answering that I only believe in a person's greatness if he is recognized as great by the people who know him, because if you manage to communicate something truly important, even if it is only to the small group around you, you can be sure that that light will forge its way through a whole horizon of shadows, just as the glow of a distant star travels thousands of years of darkness to reach us.

'And as for people,' I added emphatically, looking

him in the eye, 'I'm convinced that the ones we're destined to meet will always cross our paths. It's up to us to spot them, though, to tell them apart from the rest.'

And that was how the Young Prince decided to change the way he dressed. When we came out of a little shop in the town, he was wearing kids' clothing, trainers and a cap put on backwards, the golden curls of his beautiful hair poking out. You couldn't have picked him out from a thousand other boys of his age.

'When all's said and done, you were born a prince,' I concluded with a smile, hoping to make him feel special on his first outing into our world of marvels and misery.

But he answered, 'We're all born princes; it's just some don't know it and others forget…My kingdom only exists in me.'

And he ran and kicked a ball that had rolled away from a group of boys who were playing in the street, with Wings following him and nipping at his ankles.

And at this point, dear reader, I must ask you and the Young Prince's friends to forgive my interference, because from now on it will be impossible to identify him by sight alone. I know, however, that anyone who keeps an open heart will recognize him every time.

Chapter Fourteen

When we were back on the road, the Young Prince turned to me and asked, 'Please tell me how you managed not to turn into a serious person.' It seemed the idea that growing up would involve this sort of change was really preoccupying him.

'I'd started to tell you,' I said, 'that some people leave their dreams and ideals behind so that they can focus on owning more and more, as though security came from power and possessions. For some, the search for recognition and success is about escaping into the future, because they haven't had the courage to be themselves, or face criticism and disapproval, and follow their true calling. Others are obsessed with control, and they manipulate and reorder reality in relation to themselves. They judge and characterize others, stuffing them into physical and mental niches that will be very hard to ever get out of. And so they paralyse the unlimited transformative richness of the universe and of human love. If parents put as much effort into teaching their children love as they do into exacting discipline and routine, this planet would be a wonder-ful one to live on.'

'D'you mean that all discipline isn't a good thing?' asked the Young Prince.

'What we nor-mally mean by "discipline" is imposing our human, limited sense of order on to nature, which is divine and therefore superior. Humankind should beware arranging nature for their own benefit, as the result tends to be the opposite of what they intended: a natural disorder which turns against them. The pollution of the planet, the extinction of animal and plant species, the exhaustion of natural resources and many other things I could

name are negative examples of human order and discipline.'

'I understand what you're saying,' the Young Prince said, nodding thoughtfully. 'On my last trip I met a man who thought he controlled the stars. He would spend his days counting them and doing sums, and then he'd write the answers on a little piece of paper and keep it in a drawer. He thought that if he did that, he owned them.'

'I see you've noticed how much serious people love numbers. They're never satisfied,' I continued, 'until they know the exact height of a mountain, the number of victims of an accident or how much money you earn in a year, just to mention a few examples. Actually, we own nothing at all except ourselves.'

'I've heard that on this planet they also keep track of people by giving them numbers,' he said nervously.

His remark made me think about passport numbers, social security numbers, phone numbers, credit card numbers…

'That's right. There are so many people on Earth that there doesn't seem to be any other way we can identify ourselves. Names don't seem to be enough,' I replied, a little sadly.

'Show me where you keep your numbers,' the Young Prince said curiously, expecting me to uncover some part of my body.

'Oh, we don't have them stamped on to us,' I answered with a smile, as I took out some of the cards in my wallet. My face fell a little as I recalled some appalling examples of exactly the thing I'd just denied, situations I would scarcely be able to explain to him. 'Perhaps, not too far in the future,' I ventured, thinking aloud, 'our genetic code will be used to identify us all, like a unique, personal key. I hope to God that the result won't end up restricting the liberty of every human being.'

'What d'you mean?' asked the boy, noticing the concern in my voice.

'I mean that God created man and woman as spiritual beings, with a spark of free will, self-awareness and that ability to think and imagine that we call a soul. That's why, as humans, we can't give the best of ourselves, things like love and creativity, if we don't have our freedom.'

'God? Who's God? You talked about him before as though he caused a lot of the things that happen down here, or as if he were capable of sorting them out.'

'Who is He? I don't even know if we should ask who or what He is.'

'But you talk about him –'

'Well, yes,' I interrupted. 'How would I not talk about Him?' I took a deep breath, and let a few minutes pass while the Young Prince looked at me in amazement. 'If I knew what God was, I'd know everything. It's been said that He is what He is, His own beginning and His own end, and so the beginning and end of everything that exists. Others have imagined Him as a never-ending resurgence, an infinite succession of causes and effects. Some define Him in accordance with our ideas of perfection, as Goodness or Beauty; or they name Him the Word, the Creator, Truth and Supreme Wisdom.'

'So you could say,' my travelling companion came back, 'that there is more men don't know about God than they do know...'

'That's what I think, given that our limited human intelligence is unable to conceive of an infinite idea. The thing I find most shameful is that even today, in their ignorance, people carry on killing each other over the different answers you can give to that question.'

That seemed to give the Young Prince a fright, so I reassured him with a smile. 'Don't worry, I'm not that cruel!'

'And are there other questions people fight over too?' he asked, curious to know what awaited him on our intolerant, violent planet.

'There are lots, but none that has whipped up as much hatred as questions of the divine, which goes to show how little our minds have developed. Although lately, something even worse has happened: people have stopped asking themselves who God is, in the quiet spaces of their minds, as if it no longer mattered to them why they're alive.'

'And what do you think?' he asked me, hoping I'd shed a bit of light on such a clouded, confused matter.

'I prefer to feel God as a need to come together with all living creatures, as a sort of loving energy that sustains not just all of us but the whole universe. He speaks to me in a language of signs, symbols, miracles and coincidences, and that guides me along the way. Telepathy, dreams, intuitions, premonitions and all kinds of natural phenomena, like omens, hunches or visions, are a channel of communication that is always open to the alert, awakened mind and allows the transformation and full realization of the self. Sometimes it takes the form of a voice, murmuring inside me like angels; sometimes it's a storm, or a strong wind or a rainbow. If you can silence your mind, ask your questions clearly and stay alert, the answers will come. They always do!' My words seemed to reassure him. He thought for a minute in silence.

'I suppose animals can't give the best of themselves either if we shut them up in cages,' the boy wondered aloud, perhaps remembering the sheep shut up in its box, as he ran his fingers over Wings' sleeping head.

'There are people who shut their children, or others, in cages with bars made of their demands, their expectations and fears,' I reflected. 'And they don't realize that anything imposed as an obligation will always provoke resistance. Anything leading to stagnation and lack of spontaneity like that runs counter to the renewal that characterizes life. After all, we know there's nothing as static and orderly as a graveyard.'

'So we don't need orderliness?' asked the Young Prince, still unsure about this.

'There's an external orderliness that we need to feel comfortable, and we all need a different amount. But the one that really matters is the orderliness of the spirit, which should point towards God, because it's from Him that we came and it's towards Him that we're going. It's not a fixed aim, though, but rather the constant growth and evolution of our spiritual being.'

'How do you know so many things?' he enquired, surprised at my ability to find answers to his questions.

'Thanks to my experience and my intuition,' I replied.

'And how do you know you're right?'

'Thanks to my experience and my intuition,' I said again.

'And you're never wrong?' he asked admiringly.

'Of course I'm wrong sometimes, and when I am I add that error to my experience. You see, I can't tell you that something I think is a universal truth – it will just be knowledge that has been useful to me in life. And you should do the same. Don't believe what I tell you. Just take it and see if it's of use to you.'

'And where can I find that experience?' the Young Prince wanted to know.

'In life,' I replied. 'My experience is made up of all the mistakes I've had time to make, and my ability to overcome them. If you're smart, you'll be able to learn lessons from other people's mistakes without having to repeat them yourself. Books, teachers and other people's stories can show you the way, but in the end it's you that has to decide what knowledge you will take on.'

When I saw his expression I realized that all this was sounding a bit vague to him. I have no doubt that young people learn more from our examples than from our words.

We were on a stretch of road that runs alongside a deep ravine, with a river snaking along the bottom. The strange, jagged outlines of the Andes rose up on both sides. One in particular caught our attention: a tall spire of rock that stretched up from the crest of a hill towards the sky. A sign told us it was called 'The Finger of God'. I smiled as I thought of the locals rushing to give it a sacred name before travellers came up with other resemblances.

Personally, I found it easier to imagine, as Michelangelo had in the Sistine Chapel, that God's finger reached down towards humanity and not the other way round. At that moment the answer I'd been looking for popped into my head.

'Experience,' I said, and my friend turned towards me, 'is like a map. Although it's an unfinished map, sadly, when it comes to the future. That's why every day you should affirm all of your assumptions that have turned out to be correct, and discard any that are wrong.'

'And what about intuition?' asked the tireless Young Prince. Clearly, no one inside that car was about to congratulate me on the aptness of my analogies.

'Intuition gives you your first impression of a person or a situation. And it's usually right. Unfortunately, our society has overestimated rational, deductive reasoning, which is slower; and although it can be useful in science, it's harder to apply to human questions. Intuitive knowledge, on the other hand, is immediate and complete.'

'I think my flower was intuitive,' he said, 'because she knew things before I told them to her. Perhaps that's why people and flowers sometimes don't get along.'

Chapter Fifteen

I felt utterly immersed in the pleasure of driving down that sinuous road, which now hugged the shore of a lake nestling in the pine forests. With each gear change, the engine's sonorous strum vibrated up my spine. At such a special moment for a lover of cars and speed, the boy's sudden interjection was bound to fall on me like snow in spring.

'You were telling me about serious people,' he reminded me. 'What else do you know about them?'

'A few things,' I murmured lazily, deciding it would be pointless to explain to him that he'd just interrupted a unique mechanical symphony. 'I very nearly became a distinguished member of that species myself, after all.'

'And what stopped you?' probed the Young Prince,

who always found his way to the crux of the matter.

'When I really looked at the serious people around me – all respectable, successful types – I realized that none of them was truly happy.'

'Don't tell me that order and discipline made them unhappy,' he pleaded. 'Was that it?'

'No,' I replied. 'What happens is that most serious people who like order hate surprises and anything else that's beyond their control. But the more control they exert, the less they enjoy it. They like to live in a world that moves along a nice, predictable orbit – a world without magic or delight. Changes, however small, have them all worried and upset, and our unstable reality contains countless opportunities to be both.'

'What you're saying reminds me of a lamplighter who was incapable of varying his routine,' explained the Young Prince. 'When his planet started to turn faster, his work became a torment.'

'Well,' I continued, 'those people's passage through life is as sparkling and brief as their epitaphs, however many medals and diplomas they've piled up. No one dares to put a footnote at the bottom of a tombstone saying, "And in spite of it all, he was never really happy." With shooting stars, the sky writes on its vault the eulogy they deserve.'

'No one should congratulate themselves on being a shooting star,' he mused.

'No, that's right,' I agreed. And I added, 'They're like little flames that flare and die. Fireflies in the evening of time.'

I continued with my reflections. 'And then there are those other people who, when faced with reality, can't let go of their ideals (like the serious people they are), who try so hard to protect those ideals that they end up building a wall around them, and all they manage to do is suffocate their spirit. Sometimes that wall is so perfectly built that they can't find a single crack to climb back through. And so they get stuck outside, like puppets with no strings to animate them, like ghosts that don't know who they are, where they've come from or where they're going. Their planets stray without direction, and with time they become as cold as wandering comets.'

'I don't want to be a wandering comet,' stated the Young Prince. Then he asked, 'What is a ghost?'

'A ghost is an empty image, a shadow, a shell with no substance. There are people who don't think ghosts exist,' I added. 'But I'm quite sure they do, and there are a lot of them, everywhere you go. For me, ghosts are people with no heart.'

'I don't want to be a ghost either,' the Young Prince said, becoming more and more conscious of the difficulties that growing up would involve.

'In that case, don't betray your desires, and don't bury them inside yourself until they die of starvation. Learn to bring what's real together with what you yearn for. In all that you do, give the best of yourself so that your spirit is returned to you, and offer the best of yourself to each person so that they can return your love. You'll see that the world will become a magnifying mirror, reflecting back at you everything that you gave without self-interest, and more. Because the only way to surround yourself with smiles is to smile, and the only way to surround yourself with love is to give it to others. There will come a moment when you're suspended between a world that revolves around you, in childhood, and a world that is open to others when you're grown up. It's then that you have to let go of everything fanciful, all your stubbornness and all your selfishness, so you can grow into the convictions you'll need for defending your noble ideas. Love yourself, and you'll be able to love others. Love your dreams, so that you can use them to build a world that is warm and beautiful, full of smiles and hugs. That will be a world you want to live in, and it will turn in the orbit of a rainbow. If you really believe in it, and build it up bit by bit with every little act, that world will become real for you. And it will be the reward for all your worthy endeavours – I've never seen someone fully enjoying an undeserved happiness. It's only people who truly love that are like stars, and their light keeps shining on us after they are gone.'

It seemed to me that his voice glowed with feeling as he said, 'When I die, I want to be a star. Teach me to live so that I can become a star.' Cradling his dog, he leant his head against the window.

'There's no exact formula I could teach you,' I replied gently. 'I'm not a master of the stars. All I can offer you is what I've learned in life – a handful of truths that, like all truths, can only be communicated with love. Like all of us, you've got the capacity to love, and that's all you need. Whenever you have doubts, search inside yourself, and if you're patient enough, you'll always find the answer.'

But he was no longer listening...Perhaps he discovered that in the land of dreams, we can all be princes and stars.

Chapter Sixteen

That night we stayed in a beautiful guest house that sat surrounded by a great forest on the shore of a lake. It was a simple building of wood and stone, with lovely fires burning in the grates. The walls of the rooms were papered with patterns and colours inspired by the rooms' names. Ours was called 'The Meadow': it was bright green, and the prints were of plants and wild flowers. The rules of the place meant that Wings had to sleep alone that night, in a small but comfortable room. Even then I feared it would be hard for my friend to be separated physically and emotionally from that puppy.

I shouldn't have been surprised when, as I went down to the dining room for dinner, I found the same noisy family we'd seen at lunchtime – the hotels aren't exactly numerous around there. As was perhaps to be expected, our entrance caused the same hubbub as it had done a few hours before, proving that some people never change. But as dinner went on, perhaps because both children and adults were tired, the atmosphere at their table became so unpleasant that the barely contained aggression and violence started to make us quite uncomfortable.

The youngest child was crying inconsolably. Another wasn't allowed to eat his dinner as a punishment. A third was being forced to finish a plate of fish that he clearly didn't like. The other two stared straight down at their plates, not daring to pass comment on their brothers' predicaments. All of this had such a profound effect on my young friend, unaccustomed as he was to family arguments, that he seemed to lose his appetite. And then came our journey's second miracle of love: he got up from the table, went to get Wings and, carrying him in, wrapped in his arms like a soft white baby, gave it to the children as a present. Their eyes were wide with joy as they all reached out to stroke the puppy.

The Young Prince's gesture and attitude were so moving that the parents were speechless. By the time they could react and try to return the gift (no doubt with all kinds of sensible reasons), Wings was already a part of their life. They just about managed to look at me, as if I was the father and needed to give my consent. When I smiled and nodded, it was a done deal. The next day there would be eight of them on the road together.

A happy feeling returned to the dining room then, and my young friend was able to enjoy his food, though he was frequently interrupted by the children's shouts and laughter, and barks of delight from Wings, who now had five masters to play with him and satisfy his every need.

'It's quite wonderful that you were able to do that, especially with children who were laughing at you just this morning,' I remarked, to see how he'd react.

But he replied, 'You helped me realize that I provoked them with my strange appearance, and that it's normal for children to react spontaneously. Also, I couldn't stand the tension much longer and I felt I had to do something to relieve it. And I had Wings, who had brought me happiness when I most needed it. It feels right that he can make others glad now.'

With this heart-warming experience, the second day of our journey came to a close. Once again, I felt that the Young Prince had cut through all my wordy explanations.

Chapter Seventeen

I woke up a little later than usual, after a restorative night's sleep. I looked over at my room-mate's bed, but he wasn't there. When I opened the curtains, I saw him down by the shore of the lake, standing alone and still as the water itself. The first rays of sunshine were drying up the last wisps of a cloud, like candyfloss melting in a child's mouth. The whole landscape radiated a sense of immense peace.

We got on the road again after eating breakfast. As we left, we noticed that the noisy family's car was no longer there. After a quarter of an hour driving down a dirt road in the shade of cedars, araucarias and fir trees, we were approaching the edge of the forest.

Quite without warning, the Young Prince shouted, 'Stop, please!'

'What's wrong?'

'Please stop the car!' he repeated, clearly worried about something.

As soon as I did so, he got out and ran twenty yards or so into the wood without a word.

Oh, so that's what it was about, I thought to myself with a sigh of relief, surprised that my friend's bodily needs would assail him so suddenly.

But then I

discovered bitterly that that wasn't what had made him cry out. Unlike on the first day, when he had walked towards me with shining eyes, now it was with a look of pain and disappointment that he came back holding Wings curled up in his arms.

I could hardly believe that someone would abandon such a gentle creature.

Wings was nervous with fright, whimpering and trembling as he licked desperately at the Young

119

Prince's hands. It couldn't have been clearer how happy he was to see us again.

'It can't have been the children,' I offered, trying to guess how my friend would feel, faced with such cruelty. 'I don't understand why they didn't leave him at the guest house so that we'd get him back. Just a note of thanks or apology would have been enough,' I complained, while the Young Prince remained silent.

All the excitement had left the puppy weak, and as we drove off again he fell asleep in the Young Prince's lap, where the boy carried on stroking him for a long time.

Once again the road left the valley and took us into a barren landscape that was more conducive to thought than conversation.

Neither of us dared to break the silence, as though there were no words appropriate for the situation.

Eventually I said, 'Let's be thankful that Wings is still alive. Let's forgive them and put it behind us.'

The Young Prince was silent, as though he hadn't heard me. He was melancholy and reserved.

After a long while, he said, 'I abandoned a flower, too, and I can't forgive myself for leaving her to wilt. And I feel guilty for having doubted my friend's good intentions, although the tuft of grass is partly to blame for that.'

I understood then what had been keeping him trapped in the past, casting a shadow over his shining smile.

'That's the difficulty that's preventing you from moving forwards,' I announced, utterly convinced of my diagnosis. 'Listen carefully, because I'm going to tell you the secret of happiness.'

'You know the secret?' asked the Young Prince, opening his eyes, scarcely believing that the answer humanity had been searching for for centuries was about to be revealed to him.

'Well, yes, I think I do,' I replied, knowing that in a situation like that it's better to be sure than to feign modesty. 'I haven't deciphered some ancient manuscript or found my way into the forbidden chamber of a mysterious pyramid, but I'm convinced that this truth, like all great truths, is simple and self-evident.'

'Then tell me what it is – please,' begged the Young Prince.

'You'll be happy if you love and forgive, because then you'll be loved and forgiven in turn. You can't forgive if you don't love, because your forgiveness will never outgrow your love. And finally, it's impossible to love and forgive others without loving and forgiving yourself first.'

'But how can you love yourself while knowing your own flaws?' he objected.

121

'The same way you love others while knowing theirs. People who wait for the arrival of a perfect being whom they can love go from one disappointment to another and end up loving no one. But to love and forgive yourself, it's enough just to want to become a better person, and to accept that you have always done the best that you could.'

'And how can I know that I truly love if I've never experienced love before?' asked the Young Prince, quite logically.

'Your love is true when you put someone else's happiness before your own. True love is free and knows no limits. It doesn't seek to satisfy its own needs, but concentrates on what's good for the loved one.'

'I still don't understand how I can give that sort of love without ever having received it,' he implored.

'That's a very good point. Some humans are lucky enough to get the unconditional love of their parents. Others, through meditation, will realize that we possess immortal souls, and will sense the love of the Creator. There are people who read the gospels and feel that Jesus loved the whole of the human race with absolute perfection, so much so that He gave His life to free us from our fear of death and teach us that we are all spiritual beings rooted in our human experience. Others still will discover, through the words of enlightened teachers, a total compassion for all living creatures. If you search truthfully, you will end up finding a reason to love yourself, and you will discover that you are a unique and wonderful being.'

I was talking with great conviction, putting all the energy I could find into my words, aware that there is no mission more complex, but also none more sublime, than healing a sick heart. He listened, absorbed in a deep and respectful silence.

'We could learn a lot from children,' I went on. 'They are quick to forgive – if they weren't, life would

be one long stream of hatred and endless feuds. Anyway, what's so terrible that you need to blame yourself for? Doubting? Even the people with the firmest faith in the world have experienced doubt. Accept your mistakes and trust in God's mercy, because He has already forgiven you. And if you're not sure God exists, ask yourself what you gain by not forgiving yourself. What's more, you followed the voice inside you, just as you should, when you went in search of your aviator friend to ask him why he gave you a box that couldn't possibly fit a sheep inside.'

The boy remained silent. He was quite still, his eyes half closed. He had even stopped stroking Wings.

'And I don't think you should judge yourself too harshly for neglecting your flower. Flowers wilt with the end of the summer and bloom again in spring. Perhaps she managed to push you away, subtly, so you wouldn't see her petals wrinkle up and fall.'

I felt the full force of the Young Prince's gaze on me, as if his very life depended on each word.

'OK, so you may have left your world behind, but you did it so you could explore a bigger one. Every choice is a death, as they say. Any change means leaving a part of ourselves behind: it's the only way to grow and make progress. It's painful, but we know

that the experience will enrich us. As we go, little by
little we let go of everything dispensable and hold on
only to what is essential, like pilgrims on their way
to the shrine feeling weighed down by anything they
don't truly need.'

The words came tumbling out, guided by some
mysterious certainty in me.

'And as for the tuft of grass, don't forget that you
were going to pull her up. Your prejudices made you
believe that all grasses are weeds because they invade
the territory of flowers and men. Can you be sure
that the tuft of grass was bad in herself? You can't,
because she was doing no more than what she was
created for – being grass. Can you blame a creature
for resorting to any method of survival when its existence is threatened?'

This time the boy looked at me in amazement, but
his lips were pressed shut.

'I don't think that things are good or bad in themselves, except in relation to our needs and how we use
them. But if I had to choose, I would say that, given
they exist, they must be good. In the universal design
of creation, it's possible that a lot of things that happen
have a meaning we still haven't understood. Could it
be that weeds grow so that we have to pull them up,
and so avoid becoming lazy? Might there be pain in the

world so that we can love and value our happiness? Does hate perhaps exist so that we can experience the spiritual fulfilment of forgiveness? The truth is that without difficulties along the way, it would be impossible to make progress as human beings and discover our true nature. It is at really critical moments that the best of us comes to light.'

I took a deep breath and allowed our morning's journey to continue in silence.

It takes time for us to experience fully a true wish to forgive. Some think, paradoxically, that when they forgive, they are bestowing a benefit on someone else, when in fact the person who benefits most is the person forgiving. Negative sentiments will always turn against the person who harbours them, meaning that when we fail to forgive, when we envy and hate others, it is ourselves that we are hurting.

Suddenly, a saying of the Buddha's leapt into my mind like a hare running across a road: 'He who hurts me will receive in return the protection that comes from my love; and the greater his cruelty, the greater will be the kindness he receives.'

Chapter Eighteen

At around midday we arrived in a city well known for its leading hotel and conference centre.

They had built it to boost tourism in the region and show off the attractions of the area with business and arts conventions. We'd stopped there to have lunch, and on our way to the cafeteria we saw through an open doorway that the main conference hall was packed with people.

I looked with faint interest towards the stage, and saw to my surprise that the speaker was the father of the family we'd met the day before. He was rounding off a speech to put himself forward as a candidate, although we couldn't tell what post or duty it was for. His words struck us when he said, 'You can trust me.

I won't let you down.'

Then his eyes met the clear, piercing gaze of my friend the Young Prince.

I was overcome with an almost irresistible desire to unmask him in public, to tell everyone that he had let us down that very morning when he abandoned a defenceless little puppy.

I noted with disgust that the man's face showed neither guilt nor shame – perhaps because those feelings require a scrap of humanity.

There was no trace of resentment or hardness in the Young Prince's expression, though – only a glow so bright that no shadow could have eclipsed it.

We decided to slip quickly into the cafeteria in case their polite applause got the audience's appetite up.

We were about to start eating when the man came in and, seeing us, headed straight for our table. Surprised that he had the nerve to address us, I felt myself becoming tense.

He, on the other hand, seemed calm and relaxed. He smiled when he reached us and, putting a hand on the Young Prince's shoulder, said, 'That was a wonderful thing you did last night. And I understand quite well why you might have regretted your decision – he's a very special dog. Although I admit that the children were very disappointed this morning when they found he was gone...'

'I don't understand...' I said, shooting a quick look at the Young Prince, who stayed where he was sitting, steady and still. 'What d'you mean, they found he was gone?'

But the father, ignoring the interruption, went on. 'If you'd at least left a note saying, I don't know, how much you love the puppy, it would have been much easier to explain to the children that –'

'Look here,' I said in a more forceful tone, unable to comprehend why he was being kind and understanding, when that role should have fallen to us. 'My friend here didn't regret a thing. This morning, after you left, we found the dog in a wood and assumed you'd...'

'That we'd abandoned him?' The father completed the sentence that I hadn't dared to.

'Abandon this lovely, vulnerable, little puppy? How could you think we'd do something so cruel?' The man was defiant, and let his indignation show.

I didn't know what to say, and after an uncomfortable silence, the father continued. 'You may have seen me being strict with my sons, but I am not an insensitive person and I try never to be unjust. I simply think a bit of discipline is better than having no limits at all.' He thought about it a moment, and added, 'I don't know how it could have happened – unless the puppy managed to open the door of our room in the night, and got lost in the wood.' Then he turned to the Young Prince and said, 'Kuvaszes are restless dogs, did you know that? You're lucky you found him.'

I seemed to have lost my ability to speak, and anyway could think of nothing to say. I felt like a child caught red-handed.

'Well, I'll leave you. Have a good trip,' he said, excusing himself.

As he was walking away, the Young Prince's voice stopped him. 'Where can I find the boys?' he asked.

'In rooms 301 and 311. They'll be so pleased to see you,' he said over his shoulder, and continued towards a huge table, where people were waiting to celebrate something to do with his candidacy.

Even though I'd only known the Young Prince for a short time, I could see what was going to happen. His generosity was even greater than his love for Wings.

A few minutes later, the door to room 311 was opening and the children's shouts mixed with the puppy's cheerful yelping once more. He had got his five boisterous friends back.

At the wheel that afternoon, I promised myself that the next time I had doubts about someone, I would try and think the best of them instead of the opposite. I've realized that it doesn't matter how many times people disappoint you, because every time I decide that the next person I meet will deserve my trust and my love, I am a happier person, and the world seems a better place.

My positive expectations of people and circumstances have drawn me towards good people and good circumstances. It's as if reality wanted to gratify us, whether we expect the best or fear the worst. So perhaps the saying is true: if you aim at nothing, you'll hit it.

I glanced at the Young Prince out of the corner of my eye, and he looked quite serene. I realized that he hadn't uttered a single negative thought about that family that whole morning.

When I assumed that the children hadn't done anything, I had blindly condemned the father from the outset. And worse still, when I saw him on the stage I realized that, in spite of all my pretty words about forgiveness, I hadn't forgiven him at all.

At one point it occurred to me that the boy might have suspected the truth from the start, and had done nothing to deliver me from my mistake – but I put the thought out of my mind. Just then, the Young Prince's lips curled upwards into a bright, peaceful smile…

Soon we were rejoining the road that would take us across one more valley and into the city. Some friends were expecting me there, to make me god-father to their first son.

On that third day, the Young Prince scarcely said a word. He would listen to me and then sink back into his thoughts, as though he could feel the end of the journey coming and wanted to absorb all of my stories.

'Talk to me about happiness and love,' he asked suddenly.

'That's quite a topic!' I exclaimed with a sigh. 'I could talk more about that than Scheherazade in the *One Thousand and One Nights*. I'll try to give you an idea of what life would be with and without love and happiness, and then you can find your own way through. Experience has taught me,' I began, 'that there is no happiness without love, if you think of love as an enduring passion for life and an endless amazement at everything we perceive through our senses – whether that's a colour, a movement, a sound, a smell or a form.'

'Do you mean,' he asked, 'that we should put our love into everything we do?'

'Exactly,' I replied. 'And do it with passion, too, whether it's work, art, friendship, sport or helping others. Happiness,' I went on, 'is a balancing act that requires the satisfaction of a lot of human needs, from the most basic – such as food, shelter, activity and company – to the highest – like the quest for transcendence, love, altruism and the search for the meaning of life itself – passing by others, such as creativity, gratitude, productivity and change. Only our intelligence can satisfy these needs in a harmonious way, in line with our personalities and our purpose in life.'

'And how will I know I've attained it?' asked the Young Prince.

'Happiness,' I explained, 'isn't so much the final objective, like the terminus of a train line, as a way of travelling – in other words, a way of living.'

'A train…?' the boy started to say.

'It's not a passive feeling,' I continued, ignoring the interruption. 'Quite the opposite – it requires attention and effort every day.'

'Why do you always start by saying what things aren't?' he complained. 'It would take half the time if you didn't.' And before I had time to come back with some observation about the dual nature of our planet, he asked, 'What is a train?'

'A set of wagons pulled by a locomotive engine along two rails that we call tracks,' I answered, trying to be brief and not say what a train isn't.

'If it's difficult to get off a road,' observed the Young Prince, 'it must be almost impossible to get off those tracks.'

My silence confirmed his suspicion.

'It sounds like there's not much room to be free on this planet,' he concluded at last.

It seemed ridiculous to get bogged down in a discussion of free will just then, so I picked up my original thread. 'To live happily you have to defend freedom, but also life, ethics, self-esteem, loyalty and peace. It's the duty of all human beings who want to live better, as well as being the most honest attitude to take in the service of others.'

'What d'you mean, "to live better"?' he asked.

'To live better is to draw fully on everything that life offers, and be open to anything that might enrich us emotionally, materially or spiritually.'

I had to make some effort to stop there, and not explain that the opposite of living better is 'staying alive', which means surviving on as little as possible. He'd wounded my pride a little, and I didn't feel like explaining more to him than was strictly necessary, even if that meant not expressing myself with clarity.

'It sounds like you have to have a lot of things to be happy,' he said.

'No, you don't,' I said, contradicting him quickly. 'Happiness comes from being, not from having; from acknowledging and appreciating everything that you already have, and not rushing to lay your hands on what you don't have. Often the thing we lack can be a source of happiness, as that's what allows others to complement us. If we were perfect, if we had everything, how would we relate to each other? Someone once said that it isn't our strength that shelters us at night, but our tenderness, as it makes others want to protect us. The simplest, most direct path to happiness is making the people around us happy,' I concluded.

We were both silent for a moment. When I saw that my young friend was listening to me closely, I went on. 'As for love, I think the truest thing anyone has said about it is that you learn to love by loving. We all have the ability to offer love, even if just with a smile, as that enriches the person giving it as much as the one receiving.'

'I think this planet would be a lovely place if everyone on it greeted each other with a smile when they met,' observed the Young Prince.

'True love,' I continued, 'focuses on what's best for the other person, and doesn't think about itself. For that kind of love, which is capable of accepting anything, of forgiving anything, nothing is impossible. If we treat others as what they are, they will carry on being the same; but if we treat them as what they might become, they will realize their full potential. That's the real altruistic love, the one that perfects everything it meets and leaves nothing unchanged.'

'Even with lots of love, you can't solve everything,' replied my friend, invaded again perhaps by a yearning for his flower, left on an asteroid drifting in space, with two volcanoes ready to erupt.

'But don't forget that you can always do something,' I said. 'Loving is not giving up on what's possible. And if love is the only thing you have left, you'll find that it's more than enough.'

'It must be very sad not to be loved,' he mused.

'It's sadder to be incapable of love,' I pointed out. Then I added, 'Some see evil as a powerful force working against love. I think the worst thing you can suffer is to stop loving. Lovelessness is hell.'

'And what happens if you make a mistake, and fail in love?'

'We learn from mistakes, so I don't see them as failures. The only real mistake is not going back and trying again and again, in different and creative ways, because if you limit yourself to repeating things you've done before, you'll only be given what you've already got. But you can't fail in love. The only mistake is to stop loving.'

'And how do I know who deserves my support and my love?' asked the Young Prince.

'Often we withhold our support so we can give it only to those who deserve it. That's a big mistake, because it's not for us to judge the merits of others, which apart from anything else is extremely complicated. We must only love. Just as with forgiveness, the person who loves most is the one most enriched by it. In the end, if God loves all human beings equally, who are we to exclude some and choose others? Pity anyone who takes advantage of your kindness. Ultimately,' I said, 'if you dedicate your life to finding the best in people, you'll end up finding the best in yourself.'

'And the fear of death,' he said unexpectedly, 'doesn't that stop you being happy?'

'Many people worry about the end of their lives. They would do better to worry about giving their lives a proper beginning, and making sure they bear fruit. I don't think we lose our souls when it happens, but eventually we all meet our fate. If we're judged when we get there, I'm convinced that the question will be: "How much have you loved?" They won't ask us "How much have you earned?", but "How much have you given to others?" Being impressive means nothing if it hasn't been in the service of others.'

After a short pause, and barely containing my feelings, I added, 'Do you know something? Love is more powerful even than death. I had a brother – he loved his wings, which were made up of many colours. They say that he died, but he lives on in our hearts. Ever since then I've thought that the ones who are really dead are those who have never loved, and those who have given up trying.'

Chapter Nineteen

We had come now to the outskirts of the city, where my friends would be waiting for me. Nobody would be waiting for the Young Prince, though – not even on his own planet. The thought made me sad, so I invited him to stay on with me.

'Life has given me so much,' I said, 'and I'd like to help you for as long as you need it.'

'Thank you,' he replied, 'but you've already done a lot...'

Just at that moment, on the way into the centre of town, we stopped at a light. A tramp came up to the car and held out the palm of his hand. As the boy lowered his window, we both noticed a strong smell of alcohol.

'Have you got any money?' asked my young friend.

'I think I'm out of change,' I answered.

'Give me what you've got, then,' he insisted.

'Are you sure?' I asked doubtfully as I fumbled for my wallet, which had got stuck in the back pocket of my trousers. 'He'll spend it all on drink.'

The light turned to green and the car behind us honked at us to move forwards, while the tramp stayed leaning into the window.

'Move over to one side and let him pass,' my friend told me, and I realized once again that it was impossible to contradict him. 'Earlier you told me we should give without asking who it is that's receiving the gift. Well, here's someone asking for our help.'

'But a guy like this, I don't think money is going to help him solve his problems,' I protested, even though I normally try and help without thinking about it.

'Perhaps some wine will help him bear them for a while, though,' he replied. 'Unless you want to listen to his story to find out what would really help him… You know what?' he added suddenly, brightened by a new thought. 'I think that's a great idea. I'm going to spend the night here. Perhaps I can do something for him, and if not, someone listening to him a bit and keeping him company is sure to do him good.'

'But you can't just stay here like that in the street,

without knowing who this man is...'

The Young Prince cut my objections short. 'Don't forget that I was also by the side of the road three days ago, and you helped me then. What's the difference? The way we look? You said yourself that we

shouldn't let ourselves be guided by appearances. You've done your good deed; now you should let me do mine. Go and meet your friends. I can be of more use here.' And then something else occurred to him, and he added, 'Come tomorrow at dawn. I'd like to say goodbye.'

The Return of the Young Prince

With those words, he got out of the car and went over to sit down beside the tramp. When he saw that I wasn't sure whether or not to start the car again, uneasy at the idea of abandoning him, he gestured for me to go on.

I couldn't stop thinking about the Young Prince and the circumstances in which we'd parted. The chances of him carrying on a rational conversation with the tramp were slim, because when someone has decided on a path of self-destruction it's very difficult getting them off it. The man might even react violently to any attempt at giving him help. But my friend was good at making the impossible seem easy – if, that is, anything were impossible for someone with such a pure heart, such a bright smile. And yet, sitting on the ground with his cap backwards, he looked just like any other child with nowhere to go.

During the celebrations, as I shared in my friends' joy, the image of the Young Prince was gradually erased from my mind, like a thorn that no longer pricks. When I went to bed, though, I couldn't help comparing my soft, warm bed to a cold, hard pavement. For a moment I thought of going to look for him, and I even got as far as leaving the room, but something told me it would be wrong to disobey his command. I opened the window. It was a pleasant spring night, although the breeze was cool. The watery light of the moon was pale next to the morning star. I looked up, once again in awe of Patagonia's star-spattered sky. Even those who know it well would still be amazed by it yet, if they only stopped to look...

Chapter Twenty

Because I'd left the window open so I'd feel closer to my young friend, the first light of dawn woke me up. I got dressed quickly and, without having breakfast, drove straight to the place where we had parted ways.

The worry I felt in the pit of my stomach evaporated when I saw him chatting with the tramp like they were lifelong friends.

'Hi!' he said, coming over to greet me, fresh as if he'd slept on a bed of roses.

'Hi!' I said back. Curious by now, I asked, 'So, what's his story?'

'He's a really good person – a university graduate, quite comfortably off. After a routine health check they diagnosed him with a terminal illness; he was given just a few months to live. He left the clinic feeling completely desperate, and, to save his family from suffering too much, decided to end his life. Luckily he didn't have the courage, or rather the cowardice, to do it, and so he started walking, got on the first train he saw and came here, where he decided to give up everything.'

A smile crept on to the Young Prince's face as he saw my look of astonishment – the solid proof that once more I'd misjudged a person and a situation.

But he went on with the story, without needing to show that he'd caught me out yet again.

'I spent all night persuading him to go back home and let his family welcome him with their love and their care, which could be a way for them to give back something of what he had given them. Even though love is not eternal, it can be given infinitely.'

'That's right,' I said, moved by the story. 'I've heard many times that those final moments in life can be more intense than all the years that have gone before. I don't think time is necessarily linear. How wonderful it would be if we could live each day as if it were our last! Think how many things we'd do; how many others we wouldn't bother with! Also, I think death comes to us of its own accord when we have learned all that we came into this world to learn.'

Finally, I asked my friend, 'And what are you going to do now?'

'Go back home with him, and stay with his family for as long as they need me. Anyway, we should never rule out a miracle,' he said, smiling. Then he added, with a wink, 'Diagnoses are wrong sometimes, you know?'

Then he gave me a hug. I felt like an electric current was coursing through me, as though every one of my nerves, arteries and cells was being charged up with new energy. For a moment, it was as though I was suspended in space.

When he let go of me, I was still feeling moved, and winked back at him as I said, 'That's right, we should never rule out a miracle.'

The tramp too seemed filled with new life, and his dirty, sad face seemed to have taken on a kind-hearted, almost prophetic look.

As they walked away, it seemed to me that they were carrying a new light with them through the streets of the still-sleeping city.

Suddenly I started to see it all a different way. I felt that it was the Young Prince, in fact, who had shown me the way with questions he already knew the answers to. I was the one who needed to resist being weighed down by my problems. I was the one who should take care not to become a ghost, or a serious person. I was the one who should feel more love for an animal than for a machine; who shouldn't cling to the past or the future but live in the present; who should forget 'having' and dedicate myself to 'being'. The one who should stop getting caught up in the means, and look more towards the end. The one who should grow in love and be happy.

My friend had limited himself in order to let me discover the best of him so that I could find the best in myself.

It was a miracle that had transformed me utterly in the space of three days, one of those marvels that no one sees coming, because miracles of love are as simple as they are great.

Tears of happiness were clouding my vision. And it was me who had to say, 'Thank you,' then, even though they were already too far away to hear me. Right at that moment, though, he turned around and smiled. Even at a distance, the flash of that white light was almost blinding. I knew that the whole universe was smiling with him.

Epilogue

This, dear reader, is the story of my journey, and I was in a hurry to write it so that you wouldn't be so sad.

I think you'll agree with me that we needn't worry so much now that the Young Prince has returned, this time to stay among us, and that life is a little more beautiful.

I haven't seen him again since that day. But now every time I smile and have reason to be kind to someone, or to do something for them, I feel as though a wave is forming. And that if the person I've helped reaches out and smiles at someone else, we become a tide that reaches every place. That's why, when I think about or miss the Young Prince, I start one of those waves, certain that it will reach him. And in the same way, since that last morning I saw him, if I'm sad and somebody smiles at me, I know that somewhere, very close by or very far away, the Young Prince has smiled.

Sometimes, as I pass by a park and see a group of children playing, I catch myself trying to spot him among them. But then I remember my own words to him: 'You shouldn't close yourself off to others because you're looking for your friend.' And I realize that I shouldn't keep looking for him, as I can see him in anyone if I remember to look with my heart.

I had spent long nights of my life going from city to city and border to border in search of a friend, until that dawn when I found him smiling in my heart...

It was a lovely spring night, although the breeze was cool. The watery light of the moon scarcely outshone the morning star...It was then I understood that I should lift my eyes to the sky!

Suddenly, something wonderful happened: the stars seemed to smile at me from on high, and when a breeze blew, they rang out like five hundred million little bells.

This book is dedicated to:

Jesus Christ, the light that guides me and the way.

My grandmother María Josefina Miller de Colman, my brother Andreas Christian, my friends Juan Ángel Saroba and Gerdardo Leone, in loving memory.

Antoine de Saint-Exupéry, for giving me the strength I needed to hold on to my innocence and the purity of my heart.

My parents, who have made love triumph over the years.

My brothers, and my beloved family and friends, because my love is multiplied as I share it with them.

My teachers, and the difficulties I encountered on the way, because by moulding and tempering my character, they allowed me to discover my spirit.

My godchildren, because they help me look to the future with joy and enthusiasm.

The Young Prince, for having another shot at happiness and not shying away from it.

My deepest gratitude goes to all those whose words and vision are somehow reflected in this work. After all the books, conversations, classes and publications, I couldn't say precisely how each one of them has contributed to my way of thinking and being. I think the best way of expressing my gratitude is to share the lessons they have taught me and that have been useful to me when I have tried to apply them. Together with my experiences, they form the foundation on which I continue to build up, day by day, my happiness and spiritual growth.